The Comet Kid

Written by Sonja Richards

Illustrated by Pauline Viall

Copyright 2007 © by Olde Towne Publishing, LLC.

Text written by Sonja Richards. Illustrations done in watercolor by Pauline Viall.
Design by Shaw & Company.

Printed in Canada.

ISBN: 978-0-9794935-0-8

The Comet Kid is an 8-year-old boy named Cody. Every July he and his family take a week-long fishing trip to their Northern Michigan cottage on beautiful Lake Tonawanda, where he has been fishing since he was three.

2

Cody is called the Comet Kid because of his love of the Mepps Comet Mino *(pronounced minnow)* fishing lure. His grandpa gave him his first one on his fourth birthday. His tackle box is now filled with all kinds of Mepps lures. He has the Black Fury, the Syclops and the Timber Doodle. Almost every slot in his box contains a Mepps. But the unbeatable lure on Lake Tonawanda is the Comet Mino.

Cody loves fishing. But he also loves his cottage and Lake Tonawanda. He often wakes up before everyone else and stands on the dock as the sun rises up through the mist on the lake. He loves the smell of the engine as it starts and hangs in the boat on those calm mornings. He loves the sound of the lure when it splashes into the smooth water. Everything about Lake Tonawanda makes him feel good.

Every year's fishing trip is exciting, but this year the Big Northern Pike Competition was being held on Lake Tonawanda for the first time. Many professional and amateur fishermen would be there to try to catch the biggest Northern Pike in the lake.

Cody did extra chores to earn the $50 entrance fee for the competition. While doing his chores he would dream of catching the biggest, meanest Northern Pike in Lake Tonawanda.

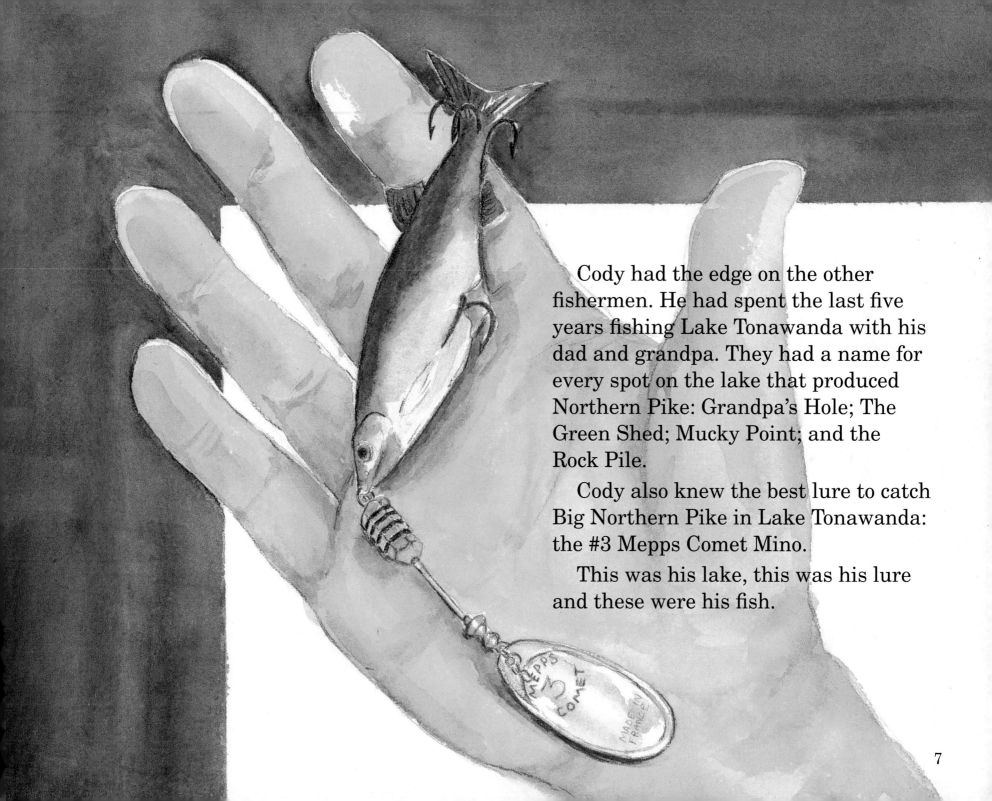

Cody had the edge on the other fishermen. He had spent the last five years fishing Lake Tonawanda with his dad and grandpa. They had a name for every spot on the lake that produced Northern Pike: Grandpa's Hole; The Green Shed; Mucky Point; and the Rock Pile.

Cody also knew the best lure to catch Big Northern Pike in Lake Tonawanda: the #3 Mepps Comet Mino.

This was his lake, this was his lure and these were his fish.

Cody's favorite fish are Northern Pike. They are slimy and long with a pointed snout filled with spiky sharp teeth. They strike hard and put up a fierce fight every time.

The toothy critters remind him of a pre-historic creature that would have been swimming during the time of the dinosaurs.

Cody could hardly wait to go after his favorite fish!

Finally the day before the competition arrived. Cody and his dad jumped into the truck and headed down to Ted's Bait Shop. Cody loved Ted's because in addition to carrying the best selection of Mepps Lures, Ted never wears shoes, which Cody and his dad always laugh about!

Ted's Bait Shop has been the same since Grandpa was a kid: cement floors; the smell of fish hanging in the air; and aisles and aisles of lures. This year Ted's shop had a different buzz to it. This was where you needed to pay your entry fee for the Big Northern Pike Competition.

Ever since Cody's very first fishing trip, he and his dad visited Ted's to get the latest Mepps lure.

"Well, if it isn't the Comet Kid!" Ted grinned as they walked into the store.

As Cody signed up for the competition, Ted gave him some advice. "Fishing is not about your age. It's about how much you love it. Good luck, kiddo."

Cody suddenly felt a little more confident. He just knew he would win.

Cody spent the rest of the day playing soccer with his sister Hannah. Just as the sun was beginning to set, Hannah went inside. Cody decided to make a couple of casts just to make sure he was ready for the next morning.

It was a calm, quiet evening. As he slowly reeled in his lure, he looked up at the first star of the night and made a wish to catch the biggest, fattest, toothiest pike in the lake.

13

SMASH! All of a sudden, his pole was nearly yanked out of his hand as a huge pike struck his lure. He reeled as fast as he could. His pole bent over, almost touching the water. Cody struggled for what seemed like forever, until just as quickly as the fish hit, it broke his line and swam away into the weedy water.

As Cody reeled in his lifeless line, his heart sank into the lake. He realized his Mepps Comet Mino was gone.

Tears welled in his eyes as he slowly walked up to the cottage. He explained what had happened. His dad looked in his box and found some Mepps, but no Comets. Cody was heartbroken. What was he going to do? Ted's would not open until well after the competition started the next day.

Just then, Grandpa walked in. "What are all the sad faces about?" They told him the story. "Go look in my tackle box," Grandpa said. "You might find something you could use."

Cody couldn't believe it! Half of Grandpa's box was filled with Mepps lures! "Grandpa, why do you have so many Mepps lures?"

"They work, don't they?" his grandpa laughed.

Grandpa saved the day! Cody grabbed a #3 Comet Mino and went to bed dreaming of what would come the next day.

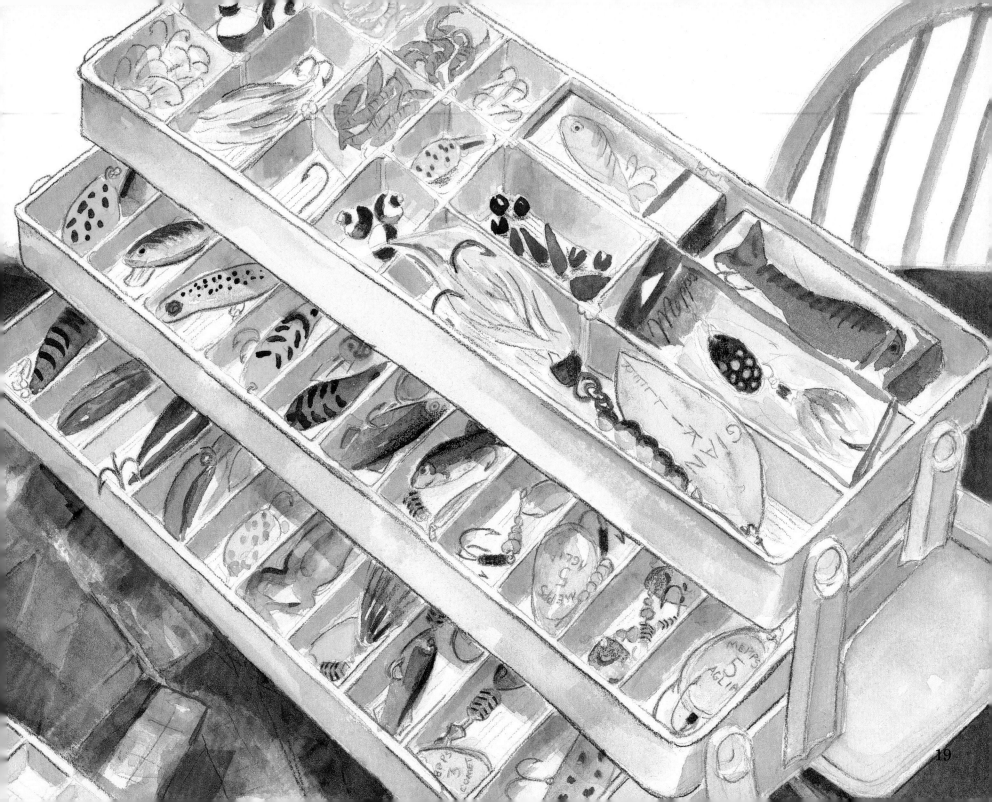

19

Cody woke up early the next day. It was cloudy, rainy and windy, and the lake was rough.

Cody was very disappointed. He sat next to Grandpa, who said, "It looks pretty rough out there today. Just remember, sometimes the worst conditions make the best fishing."

Grandpa should know – he'd been fishing Lake Tonawanda for over 50 years!

Suddenly, Cody's dad burst into the kitchen and said, "Get your gear. The competition starts in fifteen minutes!"

Cody grabbed his rain suit, pole and tackle box and sprinted to the dock. He jumped into the boat, stowed his gear, and put on his life jacket. His grandpa and dad were right behind him. In seconds they were off for the southern shore of Lake Tonawanda where the competition was to begin.

By the time they arrived, the
dock was teaming with anxious
fishermen of all ages. Some had
fancy, big boats with huge engines.
It was quite a sight!

Dad quickly signed them in. The competition would end at 5:00 sharp and was strictly catch-and-release. No sooner had Cody's dad returned to the boat and finished reading the rules, the whistle sounded to begin the Big Northern Pike Competition.

23

The boats all roared to life and took off into the lake. Cody, his dad and grandpa headed straight for Mucky Point, where no other boats went.

Dad cut the engine, Grandpa dropped the anchor, and Cody threw out the first cast. The tournament had begun.

Grandpa was using the Black Fury, Dad chose a Syclops, and Cody of course was fishing with his #3 Comet Mino.

After only a few minutes, Grandpa was the first to yell, "I got one!" Cody dropped his pole and netted the fish, a 3-pound bass. "Not what we're looking for today, but it sure was fun catching it!" Grandpa said as he threw it back.

They fished through lunch without another hit. They kept fishing for another hour after that. Still, nothing. They decided to move to the Rock Pile.

They cast into the Rock Pile over and over without any luck. The end of the competition was nearing.

Finally, it happened. Cody's pole bent to the water. The drag screamed and a giant pike danced on the surface. The monster fish was pulling their boat in a circle. Grandpa hauled in the anchor and Dad started the engine to keep them off the rock pile.

This was a huge fish! After twenty minutes, the pike finally started to tire out. Grandpa grabbed the net and scooped up the toothy critter. Its nose touched one seat of the boat and its tail the other. This was the biggest fish Cody had ever caught!

Cody's dad looked at his watch. It was 4:45. They had 15 minutes to get back to the dock. He started the engine and took off across the lake, smashing through the waves. All around them boats raced for the finish.

They arrived with just two minutes to spare. Cody grabbed his fish and headed for the weigh-in area. No one could believe the size of his pike!

Cody was the last fisherman to weigh in. Its official weight was 15 pounds, 4 ounces – 5 pounds bigger than any other fish at the tournament. Cody was the champion! His name was in the paper, he got a plaque for his wall and he won a week-long fly-in fishing trip to Northern Canada.

The best part, though was fishing with his dad and grandpa.
It was a day he would never forget.

"I dedicate *The Comet Kid* to my husband, Bret, and my children, Hannah and Cody. They are constantly inspiring and supporting me."

— *Sonja Richards, Author and Publisher.*

"This book is dedicated to the memory of my mom, Mary Alice, who always encouraged me."

— *Pauline Viall, Illustrator.*

To order your own Comet Mino or any other Mepps fishing lure, visit their website: www.mepps.com.
If you would like to receive a Mepps catalog, please call 1-800-237-9877.

If you want to learn to catch a fish like Cody, go to: www.takemefishing.org.